Also by Satoshi Kitamura

What's Inside

When Sheep Cannot Sleep

UFO Diary

Ned and the Joybaloo
Written by Hiawyn Oram

A Boy Wants a Dinosaur
Written by Hiawyn Oram

A Creepy Crawly Song Book
Written by Hiawyn Oram and Carl Davis

Paper Dinosaurs

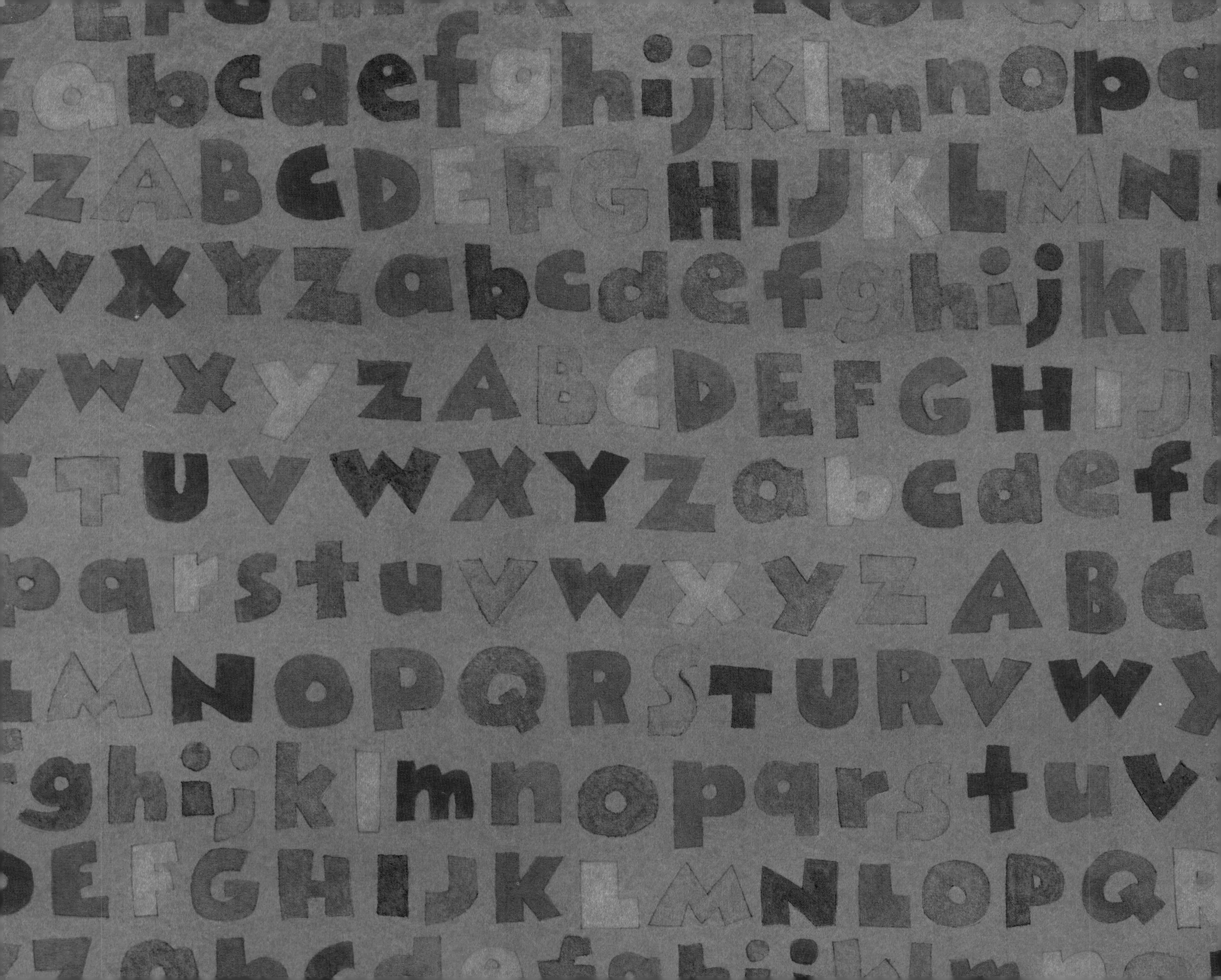

abcdefghijklmnopq
ZABCDEFGHIJKLMNO
wxyzabcdefghijkl
wxyzABCDEFGHIJ
TUVWXYZabcdef
RSTUVWXYZABC
NOPQRSTURVWX
ghijklmnopqrstuv
DEFGHIJKLMNOPQR

"From ACORN to ZOO"

AND EVERYTHING IN BETWEEN IN ALPHABETICAL ORDER

SATOSHI KITAMURA

A SUNBURST BOOK   FARRAR, STRAUS AND GIROUX

What is the armadillo balancing on his nose?

B b

brontosaurus

bus

bridge

bamboo

boat

blackbird

bench

boy

bear

balloon

bell

box

book

barrel

bottle

baby

ball

bat

butter

beaver

bag

bicycle

basket

bread

beetle

binoculars

Who's watching Baby go up, up and away?

Cc

crow
clock
calendar
Curtain
cloud
church
chimney
cupboard
Cow
camel
candle
cucumber
crocus
can
cup
cactus
carrot
chair
cherry
clarinet
cabbage
cat
cornet
cap
crayon
cage
cobra
chameleon
crocodile
cockroach

How does a cat toot a tune to charm a cobra?

Why should Dog
and Duck duck?!

egg

E e

elm

eagle

earthworm

egret

elephant

eye

ear

easel

eider

eel

envelope

Which came first, the eagle or the…?

With what feathered friend does Frog share his fruit?

What is the grinning girl holding in her hands?

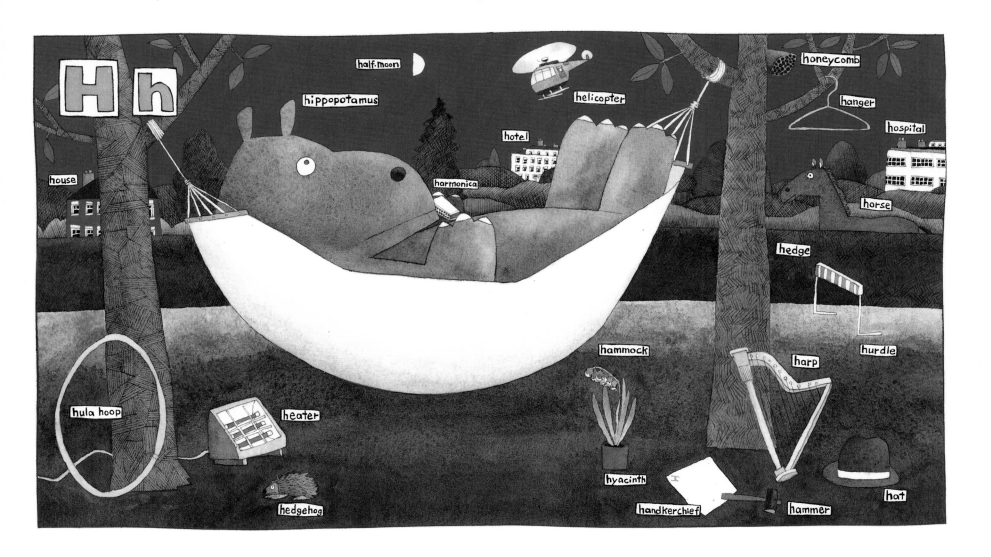

H h

half-moon

hippopotamus

helicopter

honeycomb

hanger

hotel

hospital

house

harmonica

horse

hedge

hurdle

hula hoop

hammock

harp

heater

hyacinth

hat

hammer

handkerchief

hedgehog

Who's hiding in Hippo's hat?

icicle · iceberg · ibis · island · igloo · ice cream · iron · iguana · ivory · iris · ice · insects · ice skates · ink

How does an eager iguana glide on the ice?

What will Jaguar enjoy for dessert?

"Who's sleeping in the kennel?" caws Kiwi.

L l

linnet
leaf
lantern
lake
lily
lightning
lighthouse
lamppost
lawn
ladder
lamp
lollipop
lemon
lute
lettuce
letter
lion
log

How does Lion light up the night?

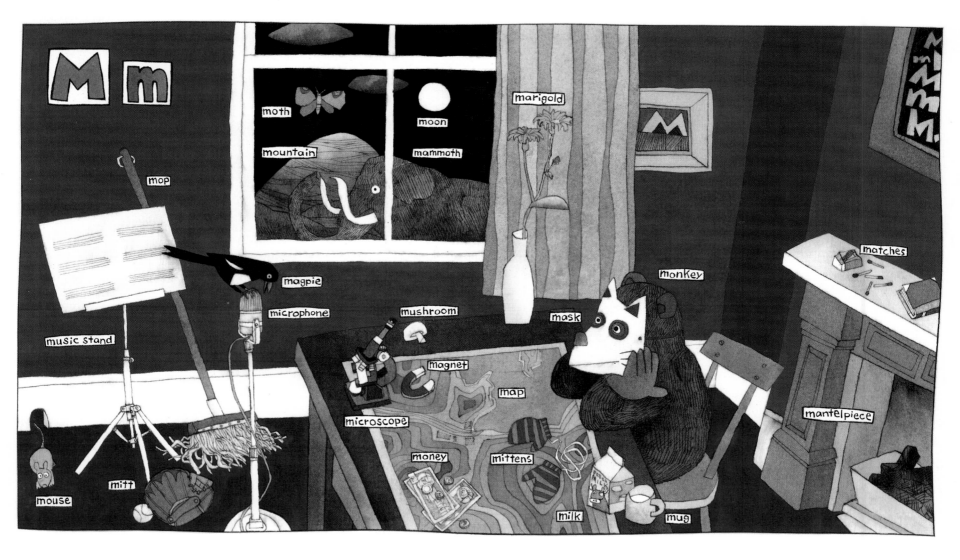

M m

moth
moon
mountain
mammoth
marigold
mop
magpie
microphone
mushroom
monkey
mask
matches
music stand
magnet
map
microscope
money
mittens
milk
mug
mantelpiece
mitt
mouse

"Boo!" says the masked magpie.
Who does he scare?

N n

nest

neon lights

NEW York

NEPTUNE

nightingale

nail

necktie

nose

notebook

net

newspaper

noodles

nut nutcrackers

nippers

napkin

nappy

What does a natty nightingale wear?

observatory

overcoat

owl

oar

Octopus

ostrich

otter

Onion   okra   orange

oboe   ocarina

Whooo goes out to
sea with Octopus?

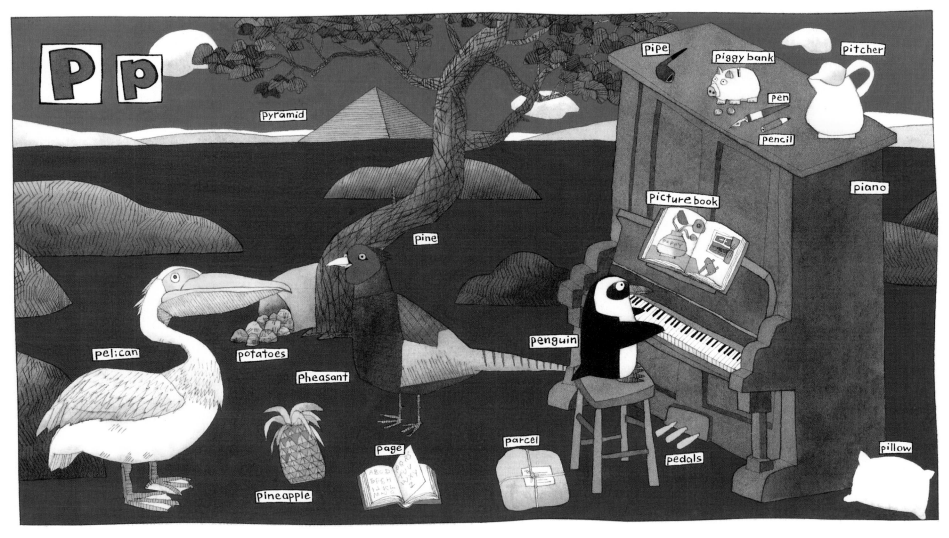

P p

pyramid
pipe
piggy bank
pitcher
pen
pencil
piano
picture book
pine
pelican
potatoes
Pheasant
penguin
page
parcel
pedals
pillow
pineapple

What is Penguin putting
in the postbox?

POST

What can a queen use to make her Q's?

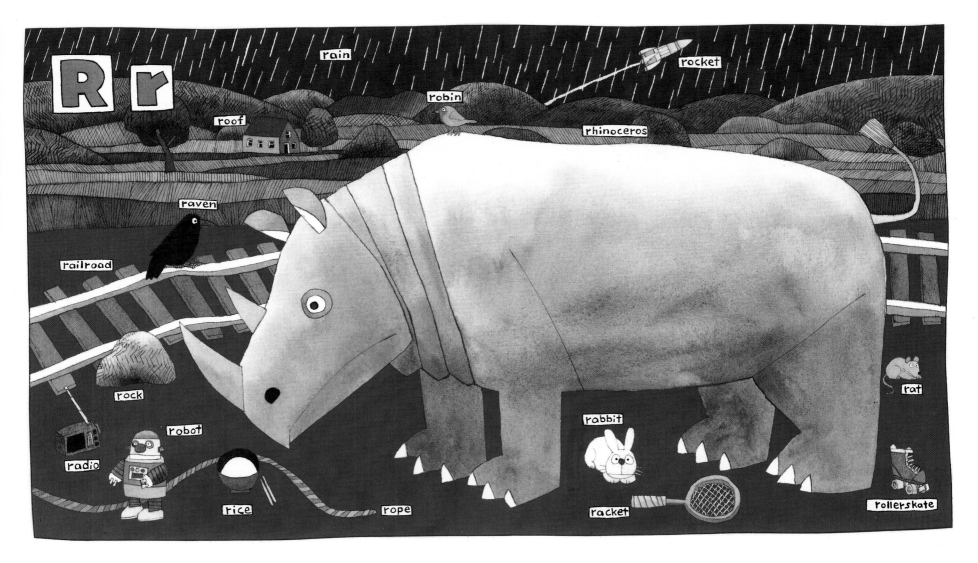

R r

rain
rocket
robin
roof
rhinoceros
raven
railroad
rock
robot
radio
rice
rope
rabbit
rat
racket
rollerskate

How does Rabbit
race along the road?

sun · Sky · swallow · sea · Submarine · Shoes · sea gull · socks · Snorkel · Sunglasses · Shark · Sea horse · Sea anemone · salmon · Sponge · Sea urchin · Starfish · seaweed · Squid

What should a snazzy sea gull wear
at the seashore?

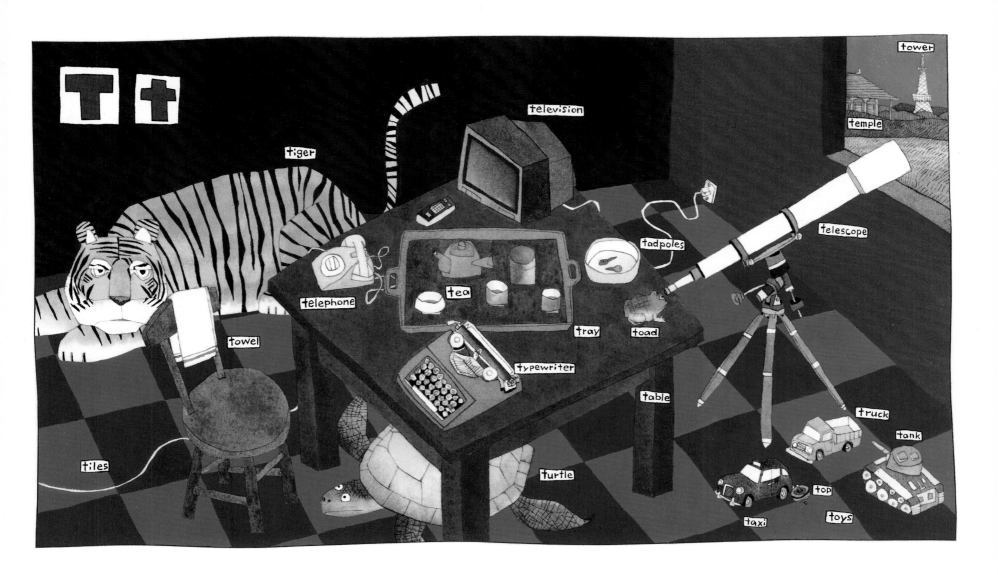

Who watches Turtle while
Turtle watches television?

Up in the sky! What's coming
to visit Unicorn?

volcano

vine

van

vulture

viper

violet

violin

vacuum cleaner

vegetables

vase

Who plays the violin
like a virtuoso?

walls
wings
warbler
woodpecker
wardrobe
wolf
whale
waves
willow
wallaby
walrus
watch
wheelchair
weasel
window
wool
wallet
walnut

What do Wolf and Wallaby
wear to keep warm?

Yoohoo! Where are Zebra's friends?

a b c d e f g h i j k l m n o p q

z A B C D E F G H I J K L M N

W X Y Z a b c d e f g h i j k

x y z A B C D E F G H

U V W X Y Z a b c d e f

q r s t u v w x y z A B C

M N O P Q R S T U V W X

g h i j k l m n o p q r s t u v

D E F G H I J K L M N L O P Q